# DC SUPER HEROES

# SUPERGIRL™

# AN ORIGIN STORY

raintree
a Capstone company — publishers for children

Raintree is an imprint of Capstone Global Library Limited, a company
incorporated in England and Wales having its registered office at 264
Banbury Road, Oxford, OX2 7DY – Registered company number: 6695582

www.raintree.co.uk
myorders@raintree.co.uk

Designed by Hilary Wacholz
Contributing artists: Luciano Vecchio, Dan Schoenin, Erik Doescher,
Mike DeCarlo, Lee Loughridge and Leonel Castellani
Printed and bound in India

978 1 3982 0602 1 (hardback)
978 1 3982 0603 8 (paperback)

**British Library Cataloguing in Publication Data**
A full catalogue record for this book is available from the British Library.

# AN ORIGIN STORY

**WRITTEN BY
STEVE BREZENOFF**

**ILLUSTRATED BY
DARIO BRIZUELA**

SUPERGIRL BASED ON CHARACTERS CREATED BY
JERRY SIEGEL AND JOE SHUSTER BY SPECIAL ARRANGEMENT
WITH THE JERRY SIEGEL FAMILY

The planet Krypton is dying. Its people didn't treat their planet well. They used all its power and energy.

"I'm scared," Kara says. She hugs her mother, Alura. Then she climbs into her escape ship.

"You will not be alone," Alura says. "Your cousin, Kal-El, will be with you. He will need you to care for him." Kal-El is launching from a different city, but their ships have the same landing **coordinates**.

"You're supposed to be a baby!" Kara says. "I'm your cousin, Kara. We were meant to arrive here together."

"I am nearly 30 Earth years old," says Superman.

"But that would mean I'm almost 30 years late!" Kara says.

"You look about 16," Superman says. "Your ship must have been knocked off course. It put you to sleep to prevent you from aging."

"That probably explains why I'm so hungry," Kara says. "I haven't eaten for 30 years!"

"We can eat soon," Superman says. "First, there's a lot to explain."

Superman tells Kara that Earth's yellow sun gives people from Krypton special powers. He leaps into the air. He soars overhead, flying with ease. Kara watches him zoom across the sky.

"Whoa," Kara says. She crouches and jumps as high as she can.

"It's working!" she shouts.

She tries to take off after her cousin. Instead, she spins in circles. It's hard to go in the right direction.

"Uh-oh," she says. She begins to zig-zag towards the ground. She tries to land, but tumbles before slamming face-first on the ground.

Superman lands beside her. "You're fine," he says. "You and I are very strong here."

Sure enough, Kara isn't hurt.

"You will need to control your powers," Superman says. "They can be dangerous." He leaps into the air again. Then he uses his heat vision to blast a nearby stone to bits.

Kara copies him. She aims for a stone. Instead, she hits a huge tree. The tree starts to burn.

Superman uses his freezing
super-breath to put out the fire.
"We'll keep practising," he says.

"With these powers," Kara says, "we could do so much to help the people of Earth."

"To the people of Earth, Superman is a hero," her cousin says.

"Then I will be one too," Kara exclaims.

"It's too dangerous," Superman warns. "There are bad people on Earth. Some of them even know how to defeat Kryptonians."

Superman explains it is important for Kara to blend in. He puts on a pair of glasses and the ordinary clothes he wears every day. He shows her his **press badge**. It says Clark Kent, *Daily Planet* reporter.

He hands Kara a set of ordinary clothes too. "From now on, you'll live a normal life as Kara Danvers," Superman says.

Kara meets Jeremiah and Eliza Danvers. They are a nice couple with no children. They know Superman's secret identity as Clark Kent. They seem kind and clever, like Kara's own parents were on Krypton. They agree to adopt Kara into their household.

After Kara has her powers under control, she starts her first day of school. She puts on a normal Earth outfit. But underneath, she wears her Krypton flight suit. It makes her feel more at home.

Kara is not sure what to think about school on Earth. Maths lessons are boring. They taught much more advanced maths on Krypton.

In PE, Kara wins every race. Everyone wants her on their team.

During history, she is completely lost. She slouches at her desk in the back of the classroom. Distracted, she uses her super-hearing. Suddenly, screaming fills her ears.

With super-speed, Kara runs down the corridor. She stashes her Earth clothing in her locker.

Then she runs outside, leaps into the air and follows the sounds of the screams.

A shopping centre is on fire. Kara uses her **X-ray vision**. All the customers and employees have escaped safely. But if the fire grows, the whole place could go up in flames. And the people outside could be in danger.

Kara crashes in through a skylight. She uses her super-breath to put out the fire.

With her super-strength, she clears a path through the building.

The firefighters rush in. They start spraying the flames.

Seconds later, Kara is back in her Earth clothes and at her desk in her history lesson.

That evening, Kara and Eliza sit on the couch. Eliza is reading the news on her phone.

"A mysterious teenage girl stopped a fire downtown this afternoon," she says. "She had powers similar to Superman's."

"That was a very dangerous thing you did, Kara," Superman says, coming to the front door. "If it gets out that another Kryptonian is here on Earth, you'll become a target."

"I couldn't leave those people in danger!" Kara says.

"Maybe Kara is right, Clark," Eliza says.

"Earth saved us when we needed help," Kara says to Superman. "We should help Earth back."

Superman sighs. "You're right," he says. "By day you will be Kara Danvers, a normal teenager."

"But when people need my help," Kara says, "I will become Supergirl!"

From that day on, Supergirl was
there to save the day.

# SUPERGIRL

**REAL NAME:** KARA ZOR-EL

**ROLE:** SUPER HERO

**BASE:** MIDVALE

Kara Zor-El escaped her home planet, Krypton, before it was destroyed. She and her cousin, Superman, protect their adopted planet, Earth. She fights crime while keeping her secret identity, Kara Danvers.

# THE AUTHOR

**STEVE BREZENOFF** is the author of more than fifty chapter books, including the Field Trip Mysteries series, the Ravens Pass series of thrillers and the Return to the Titanic series. He's also written three young-adult novels, *Guy in Real Life*; *Brooklyn, Burning*; and *The Absolute Value of -1*. In his spare time, he enjoys video games, cycling and cooking. Steve lives in Minneapolis, USA, with his wife, Beth, and their son and daughter.

# THE ILLUSTRATOR

**DARIO BRIZUELA** was born in Buenos Aires, Argentina, and as a teen he began studying in an art school – doing drawing, sculpture, painting and more. After discovering super hero comic books, his goal was to draw his favourite characters. He has worked for major publishers like Dark Horse Comics, IDW, Viz Media, DC Comics and Marvel Comics. He has also worked for Hasbro and LEGO. Star Wars Tales, Super Friends, Justice League Unlimited and Scooby-Doo are just a few of his artistic contributions.

# GLOSSARY

**atmosphere**  the layer of gases that surrounds some planets, dwarf planets and moons

**coordinates** a set of numbers used to show the position of something on a map

**crest**  an ornament worn on a uniform to symbolize or identify one's role or position

**flight suit**  a one-piece suit that protects a pilot

**press badge**  a pass that identifies members of the press and grants them special privileges

**X-ray vision**  the ability to see through solid objects

# DISCUSSION QUESTIONS

Write down your answers. Refer back to the story for help.

## QUESTION 1.

Kara struggles to master her new super powers. Has there been a time where it was hard for you to learn something new?

## QUESTION 2.

Superman tells Kara to keep her identity a secret. Why do you think it would be dangerous for people to know Kara was from Krypton?

## QUESTION 3.

Reread pages 16-22. What powers does Kara have? Which power, or powers, would you want the most? How would each power be helpful in your everyday life?

## QUESTION 4.

Why do you think Kara looks so surprised to meet Superman here? Explain your reasoning.

# READ THEM ALL!!

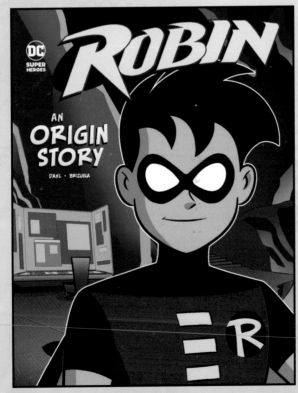

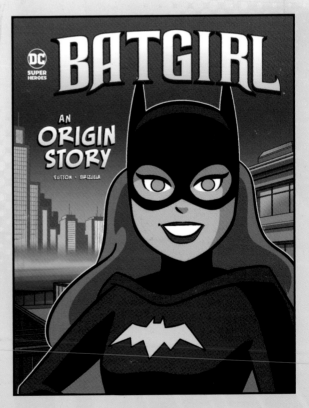